ANNABELLA

ANNABELLA

DONNA DEAL

Printed in the United States of America
ISBN 978-1-64133-672-7 (sc)
ISBN 978-1-64133-673-4 (e)

Library of Congress Control Number: 2021925050

Action and Adventure • Drama
2022.01.05

MainSpring Books
5901 W. Century Blvd
Suite 750
Los Angeles, CA, US, 90045

www.mainspringbooks.com

TABLE OF CONTENTS

CHAPTER 1

TEN YEARS GONE

I t's been ten years since the kidnapping of four women who started out so innocently investigating a group of golfers in the Gold Capital of the World, Myrtle Beach, South Carolina to find out why they were so fascinated with strippers. This devastating and dangerous event changed their lives forever. The Russian underground has constantly solicited us with propaganda concerning families of those of us who have become sex slaves to the Russian Federation Militia. They used Cybercrime to detect the whereabouts of our loved ones and follow them throughout their everyday lives. Toby, who was my superior and whom had kept me (Annette) for his own slave had named me Anna Bella, often took me to his headquarters to show me what was going on with my family. I was drugged during these times which made it difficult for me to show any emotions. Everything was a blur to my life and right before my eyes my children were growing up without me and my husband had fallen in love with someone else. Toby would often boast that he was a better man for me and show me what a man represents to his woman. He constantly made me watch video tapes of my husband making love to his girlfriend. His security forces had installed hidden cameras in my husband's bedroom. All I could wish for was one day my husband would find them and be able to trace them to the person(s) responsible for spying on him. My husband was very unaware that the woman he was sleeping with was a spy who had been sent to seduce him and take him for his money. His family were from Texas and in the Oil Company business with big investments in Crude Energy in the Texas, Oklahoma and North Dakota wells, so there was lots of money to go around to him and his siblings. When Toby discovered that I was married to a very rich man, he used it strategically to his advantage. I stayed subdued, used and abused. Not nearly the life that was planned for me in the United States of America as a happy American wife and mother raising a family and living her dream.

Naughty Nata totally disappeared to go on to far better entertainment of which the Militia had in store for her. She traveled all over Europe and soon was world renowned for her sexual entertaining abilities with the most popular members of government and especially to world leaders. The last I heard from Tina, who had become my follower outside in the real world, was the day were taken to the "Castle", which was the whoring grounds for all who performed and entertained in sadistic, tortuous sex games. You never knew if it was a day or night because we all stayed in a non-lighted environment. We were only allowed candle light for bathing, dressing, eating and reading. All other times, we were like rats in a cave, crawling all over each other. Most of the time you were not really in a thinking moment of any kind due to the amount of heroin being pumped into your body.

Toby was so possessive of me that he hardly left my side but to do his heavy training of the new comers to the Federation. It was difficult for me to even think about escaping much less making an attempt to do so. I was totally his Anna Bella and only those he approved of would be allowed to perform with me. Men and women were shot everyday by this mad man over sex and I truly would not cross his path to be shot. There has always been some hope in my heart to find a way to go back to my country, America.

Judy and Jan, my other friends who were kidnapped with me, have been beaten and raped repeatedly time after time and I have heard others say they both are like zombie in the underground begging for food and often having to participate in groups of men and women who just totally take them to their limits that almost kill them. Tina showed up the other day and told me a horrifying story that just made me scream. Judy fought back so hard last week with these two soldiers who were sharing her sexually, she actually bit part of an ear off of one. They say she is scarred for life from the chains and whips they used to beat her with. I can't believe she hasn't found a way to kill herself. I can honestly say, as bad as it has been for me these past ten years, I guess I'm lucky to have Toby, even though he still tortures me with his sadistic minded ways. It has been a living hell for four housewives from America who dared to seek information about a stripper's life and what made these nasty, naughty girls tick. Someday soon I will find a way to get away from here if it's the last breath I take trying. I really don't believe what Toby tells me that my family has given up on me. I will continue to pray for a way out of this or die trying to escape.

HUMAN MARKET PLACE

It was a very dreary, cold and damp atmosphere down here but Tina came to get me and said that Toby wanted me to start going out to the other side to see how women really get sold in this country to the public and are taken, never to be found again. He was sure this would change my thoughts I was having lately about the underground. His idea is that I am the Queen of all Queens to be treated and supported by such a superior person. His imagination soe days leaves a lot to be desired and if I had my choice I would never be his Queen Anna Bella! I would cut off his head!

I was instructed that I could not talk or make any sudden movement during the time I would be allowed to move about in the market place. There were men everywhere stalking about like wolves getting ready to snatch their prey.

Even evil looking women who were not wrapped in clothing, who had their skin, faces and bodies exposed were watching you like they wanted to devour your ever being. Smells of drugs and alcohol were also present as we strolled through the dirty street which to me look like a scene from Jack the Ripper movie.

It wasn't long before we reached a large group of women who were wrapped in clothing like mummies with ropes around them being led by guards as if they were dogs on leashes. I watched as people swarmed around them like bees to a hive. Why was Toby doing this now after all these years, introducing me to this part of the community of the underground? The purpose to frighten was definitely there but the witnessing further of their horrifying attempts to sell women as sex slaves in the market place only made me hate him that much more. More and more questions were going through my mind as I watched these women being auctioned one by one. They disrobed these women in front of everyone and let the interested parties examine their naked bodies as if they were a piece of meat. Some very disgusting men even forced sex on them in front of the devilish looking crowd who enjoyed this as entertainment. The shock of it all just threw me into an emotional tail spin and Tina grabbed me by the arm and again whispering to me to show no weakness of any kind for fear they could draw me from the crowd just as quickly to be auctioned.

It seemed like the auction lasted forever but as the street became lifeless of people and the noise and screams had settled down, I was getting the jest of it all for the first time. Money is the root of all evil and in this part of the world people would go to great extremes to satisfy their needs for it. Sex is the second root of all evil and what these bastards would do for it doesn't leave much to the imagination either. Such cruelty to the human race and to the children being raised in this cold, dark world, makes a person want to retaliate and kill the monsters!

Tina suddenly moves through these streets like a tornado touching down and pushes me faster and faster in a different direction away from the crowd. We finally reach an area where there was canvas covered military trucks and she says, "Hurry, jump into the back" and gives me a big shove. No words have been spoken by me at this point and I'm told not to say anything, but to listen clearly to everything I'm told to do. As the truck moved, I could hear a language being spoken I hadn't heard before and was trying hard to understand the nationality. There were women of all ages and they looked very scared. I too, was beginning to be frightened and very confused. Tina touched my shoulder, pointed at two women and whispers in my ear for me to take a close look at their eyes and don't make a sound when you recognize them. "Who are these women"? It's very dark and I can't quite make out the only part of their faces I can see. Suddenly before I can do anything, guns are being fired and the truck is coming to a stop. Tina grabs me and motions for the two women in the corner to follow quickly and jump from the truck and to keep our heads down. Amazingly enough the four of us all made the jumps without a scratch but knew we were still in grave danger. Tina yelled for us to stay down as bullets were flying over our heads and the truck is attacked from the front side. She also now is using a radio that I had not seen before and shouting directions at the same time for us to follow her. We were too frightened to notice the other person beside us as we ran for our lives. What was going to happen was a mystery that was about to unfold from this terrible day in the market place.

CHAPTER 3

VANISHING IN THE NIGHT

It seemed like we ran from gunshots for hours but it was not long before we were snatched up again in a green camouflaged jeep and piled on top of one another, almost in an impossible breathing position. Tina was the first to speak out to the driver in a foreign language that I was not familiar with and then she turned to the rest of us and said we could now pull down our scarves and make ourselves known to each other.

What I witnessed at that very moment was a miracle in disguise. Right before my eyes there were two very frail tired, aged and scarred women whom I once had know as my beautiful vibrant friends. How could this be possible that Tina had brought us all back together again for the first time in ten years. Jan and Judy were so thankful for this moment but it was hard for all of us to comprehend coming together and what purpose we were being used for now. We never thought we would ever see each other again, but just knew there is more in store for each of us. There had been no other life for us over these years but brutality, sex and drugs.

Suddenly we were slowing down and Tina explained that she too had been a victim in all of this mystery and that we were about to all vanish without a trace for anyone, even Toby Zobar, to be able to find us. She ordered the driver to pull slowly into this very large building and turn off his lights. As Tina's attention was on the driver, the three of us huddled together and just sobbed with tears of joy to be with each other. Judy had so many scars on her body from abuse and Jan was skin and bones from malnutrition. I was more of a kept woman by Toby and used more for his sexual enjoyment than thrown to the dogs like my two friends had experienced. Oh, don't get me wrong, I went through hell, but I was used as a personal sex slave not everyone's sex slave. Toby was very cautious about who he wanted to share me with in his drug induced sex acts. I was Anna Bella and the special entertainment was performed with a different class of people.

Tina spoke up and asked us all to listen very carefully to her instructions because we didn't have much time for this escape plan to take place. She warned us she would be hunted along with us because by now, she was sure Toby had realized we had disappeared and would be searching with his militia soldiers. I tried to get more information out of her about everything that was happening but she said we would have to wait to talk because now every second was crucial to our escape from Russia. We all were caught up in a very violent civil war between the Ukrainian's and the Russians and to get out of this country alive would be a miracle. With that said, we all just quietly awaited our instructions but fearing any moment that we all would be caught, tortured, raped, drugged or even killed! Would this vanishing act work? How was Tina going to pull this off with being one of the soldiers herself in the Milita? All of this is not making sense to us as to why Tina would turn on and betray her fellow soldiers. There is nothing we can do but pray that her plan works for all of our sakes!

We heard the sound of a helicopter in the near distance and wondered if it was about to swarm upon us with machine guns and kill us all running for our lives. We soon realized that this wasn't the case when Tina signaled for all of us to huddle together and run for our lives into the very old, damaged looking piece of metal that was about to swallow us all up under its blades and carry us to God knows where. Everything around us smelled so nasty of gun powder and smoke from the war. We were all praying that this bird would get us in the air safely.

As we were escaping into the sky in between mountains and over top of a river, I could hear communications between Tina and the pilot that were beginning to make some sense to me. Yes, Tina was officially going to get us all out of Russia, but not until she took the entire Russian Federation Militia down. We were far from getting to cross over all the terrain and territory we would have to cover to make it to an airport where we would continue our journey to America.

CHAPTER 4

BATTLING THE MILITIA

We were in the helicopter for hours before we reached a very low and flat area in between two tall rugged edge mountainous area that seemed to be able to hide this big bird for a while. It looked as if we had reached the end of a very wide flowing river that was emptying in to the sea. Other than the sound of this monster machine we were in, everything was quiet amongst us. In fact, I remember shutting my eyes and then waking up to the dead silence of no engine noise. Jan and Judy were watching me as if they couldn't take their eyes off me and wanting me to stay close to them to keep our bodies warm. It was very cold and windy and looked as if there was going to be a snow storm coming.

On board with us were five men dressed in the same uniform as Tina and that told me they must be part of her escape plan. One of them had a map spread out and the other man was drawing and explaining directions in the sand near the river edge. He confirmed we were located in the Carpathian Mountains. The others were standing guard and there was even discussion of building a fire to keep us warm and whether it would be safe and not seen by anyone because we were between two mountainous areas.

Finally, Tina told us we were going to be here for a while so we would have to stay in the helicopter and to brace ourselves for a very bad storm. The helicopter pilot would not make any attempts until daylight to fly out of this treacherous terrain. Tina announced that pro-Russian rebels had already shot down two Ukrainian helicopters and we needed to stay where we were for right now. She informed us to never turn our backs to any of these soldiers. They were still men who once were a part of Toby's video crew who enjoyed taping women performing sex acts on each other. She too was not feeling as safe and secure but felt she may be able to talk them out of any crazy ideas they may have in their heads. At this point, we were praying that Tina would not lose he authority with these other soldiers.

We watched Tina and the helicopter pilot as they were assessing the area we were surrounded by and going over the maps. Their continuing conversation about not being out of danger from the civil war dond Toby with his soldiers were beginning to scare us, but we all kept our mouths shut. The pilot announced we only had enough supplies, ammunition, and food sources to last us a few days. He insisted that his men needed to keep up their strength so they would be the first to eat and we would follow with very small portions. He advised us to get plenty of rest because as long as we slept, we would not need food. This may seem like a good plan for him but none of us agreed amongst ourselves. We knew better than to bulk on anything he had to say. We were at his and Tina's mercy and knew we weren't in a safe location entirely.

We prepared to settle in by the fire and eat military rations out of the warm cans thrown on the fire. The men had already gulped their food down and were standing watch in their positions around the camp as it began to snow. Suddenly we heard the sounds of a possible air strike and explosion off in the distance as we scrambled for the helicopter to shelter ourselves. The pilot ordered the soldiers to climb the rocks to get a better view and told Tina to prepare everyone for a possible emergency lift off while he removed snow from the blades that already had accumulated on them. In the meantime, the soldiers had encountered a group of what appeared to be part of the Russian Federation Militia. Was it Toby and his soldiers? How did they find us so fast? The five soldiers prepared to come down off the rocks and scramble for the helicopter as the pilot ordered them too. We were now firing up and heading out through this snowstorm despite the danger of this old rattle trap! As we reached the elevation we needed to get too before we could get out from between these rocky mountain sides, we heard the sounds of machine guns as they were being fired upon us. Looking down on the ground, Tina realized Toby and his men were upon us much quicker than she anticipated and couldn't figure it out until one of the soldiers on the helicopter told her that her radio she was carrying was equipped with a secret GPS and that is how he tracked her. She ordered the soldiers to return fire and yelled at the pilot to get us out of there! As we gained altitude a missile was fired from the ground, just missing us and hit the side of the mountain throwing pieces of rocks inside the open door hitting one of the soldiers causing him to fall out of the helicopter. The pilot never flinched as he got us out of the area as fast as he could and out of the reach of the militia. Tina was stunned at the loss of one of the soldiers with such a freak incident but she knew the risk to trying to get us out of Ukraine in the midst of a Civil War and now knowing that Toby could easily track her. About the time we thought we were clear the pilot said we had been hit and was losing fuel. He only hoped we could make it across this wide river to the other side where he could set the helicopter down or the alternative would be to set her down on the snow covered grassy fields on this side of the river now and hope we could move swiftly on foot to overtake a military equipped truck. In any event we were going down whether we liked it or not! At least it would take Toby and his group of soldiers a while to get to that area from between the mountainous area we just left them in. Tina was screaming to the top of her voice, "Get this damn bird down now!" The pilot agreed as he felt it descending faster than he wanted it too. It would take great control to keep it from crashing so he prepared everyone for emergency landing. He was very well trained and knew he could do a "rolling landing" where he would maneuver the helicopter and land it like an airplane. If he could get it in a hard area of grass and stay clear of the icy covered swamp, he felt he could do this. We all just prayed and held onto one another as he made his approach. Minutes later we were being tossed around as we hit the ground and the helicopter gliding into a rocky area and coming to a stop. A miracle no one was hurt!

The four soldiers left on board exited the helicopter first and scattered about to make sure everything was clear for us to get out. Tina jumped down and helped each of us to the ground because she was afraid it might explode but the pilot felt he had saved that from happening by shutting down the fuel. We could not have had a more experienced pilot!

We were all exhausted but knew we had to keep moving and leave the helicopter. One of the soldiers found a cave and said we would have to stay in it for the night. The snowstorm was getting worse and it was extremely dark and very cold now. We salvaged what we could from the helicopter and with the guidance of the men and Tina, we made it to the cave. Realizing how critical things were for us we felt that we may be captured before we could get the hell out of this country. It was difficult to sleep that night but we managed to huddle together to stay warm by the small fire.

THE CAVE EXPERIENCE

It seemed like we were back in the underground again and I couldn't sleep for fear of something or someone attacking me. Judy was restless and got up to find a place to go to the bathroom. It was still dark so she got Tina's flashlight and took off out of the cave. Two of the soldiers were standing guard for the night and had positioned themselves where no one could see them of course. Not even Judy knew where they were located. She proceeded to do her business and as she was getting herself back together, she felt two very strong hands on her shoulders and she started to scream but then her mouth was covered. The next thing she knew there was someone on top of her ripping her clothes off and had her face down on the ground. Just as Tina warned us, one of the guards followed her and proceeded to rape her.

He wrapped her mouth with a piece of her clothing and told her if she wants to live, she will do everything he tells her. Judy was unable to get away, scream or fight. All she could do was lie there as he told her that he was going to rape her and she would enjoy every minute of it and she would tell him so when he got done with her. If she didn't listen to him, he would have the other soldier standing guard come and do the same thing to her. Even though the soldiers were dedicated to Tina, she was right they were still savages when it came to sex and women. Judy was devastated when it came to another attack on her body as had been done many times before in the underground.

He finally got her to her feet and held his knife to her throat and told her she needed to keep her mouth shut and go back to sleep in the cave. Judy stumbled her way back to the cave and was sobbing as she laid down beside us. I was aware she had left but unaware of what was going on so I whispered to her to find out why she was sobbing. She told me she just wanted to get her life back or she was going to kill herself. With that comment I knew something had happened to her while she was gone. Knowing what all of us had been through I could only imagine what it was that she went through tonight.

The next morning, we were awakened by Tina to move quickly because on of the guards had noticed soldiers around the helicopter and knew we had to get moving before they discovered the cave. However, there was a covered military vehicle with them and the pilot told the soldiers to prepare to take possession of it and kill the ones around it. Tina was all for it as she wanted to kill them all from the militia that she could. She was so revengeful and rightly so! She ordered all of us to go further into the cave and hide as best as we could. She gave me a hand gun and the four soldiers took off to take over that vehicle.

We moved further and further into the cave looking for a good place to hide. We came upon a waterfall pool of water which seemed to lead to an outside source of water which I hoped would be the river and grasslands we landed near in the helicopter. We had to crawl down to get behind the waterfall which would be an excellent place for us to hide for a while. It was so cold but we knew we had no choices but to make the best of it with the couple blankets we were carrying with us. Matches, blankets, gun, a knife, a few rations and each other were the protection we had to survive. If we learned anything from this horrible experience we had been through, it was the survival process!

CHAPTER 6

BEYOND THE CAVE

It's been about four hours since we last saw Tina and the others. Not sure what to do, we decided to come out from under the waterfall and maneuver our way back towards the entrance to the cave. It took us some time to climb up the rocks inside the cave but we finally managed to make it to the top. Jan and Judy were not sure about us going back but I felt we had no choice and we do have a couple weapons so we can protect ourselves. As we approached the entrance of the cave, we could hear someone's voice and stopped dead in our tracks to access the situation. Jan was positive it was the voice of the pilot. Judy stayed back with the knife while Jan and I moved forward trying not to make noise. It was clear that it was indeed the pilot and as we approached him, we could see he was hurt and was begging for someone to help him. Jan bent down and applied pressure to a gunshot wound to his shoulder and tore a piece of her clothing to wrap it. He was coherent enough to tell us he was unsure where everyone else was but that the truck had not moved. He was sure that most of the militia were killed but he was unable find Tina and the other four soldiers. About the time we were using our water ration to give to the pilot, we heard voices again coming towards us. It was Tina and three of the soldiers moving swiftly to get to us. Once they were back at the cave entrance and found the pilot had been shot, they started gathering around with good news that they took over the truck and left one of the soldiers behind to guard and prepare it for us to ride in it. Tina informed us that Toby was not part of the attack on us so they suspected he was hiding out somewhere, they wanted to hurry and help with getting the pilot back down the hill and in the covered truck so we could move onward. As I looked around, I saw Judy whom we left behind just in case there was a conflict and we needed her to protect us with the knife I had given her. She was coming toward us really fast but she had a look on her face like she was going to kill and sure enough she lunged at the soldier who had raped her the night before and stabbed him before anyone could stop her. She was like a lion attacking its prey and she managed to devour his every being by continuously stabbing him as he tumbled and rolled around the rocks. Until now no one knew why or what she was doing it for until she turned around and told everyone he had raped her and she just got her revenge. By the time Tina got to the soldier, Judy had cut his throat just as he had held the knife to hers that night. She sobbed as she told her story but showed no remorse for killing him.

Now we were down to Tina and three soldiers plus the pilot and as we all looked at each other, Tina told Judy he got what he deserved and that we needed to move on. Approaching the truck, we could hear it running and the snow was getting deeper around us making it hard for us to get moving too fast but we managed to get to the truck going in the direction we needed to go. Jan had nursing skills and started working on the pilot again to keep him alive and prevent infection. We had all made it to this far and I knew in my heart that Tina would keep her word and get us out of this God forsaken country. All we needed to do was avoid the militia along the way and our small group of brave soldiers were able so far to make that happen. It was Toby I was concerned about and his whereabouts. He was a very strong, determined, evil, corrupted and tortuous human being that would be very hard to capture.

We were moving along mountainous roads that were narrow with very deep and rugged edges that dropped off to very steep terrains. There was barely enough room for the truck to travel, much less if we had to meet another moving vehicle. Slowly approaching what appeared to be a small fishing village that we had seen on the map we could see ahead a cluster of sheep and people gathered in the middle of the road. Time was of the essence and we surely didn't need a blockage right at the critical part of our journey. The pilot was starting to bleed heavily again and Jan couldn't get it stopped so she advised the driver that we would need to get him to a doctor as soon as possible. We stopped to greet the villagers who were vey helpful to us and gave us the proper directions for finding medical help deep in the village ahead. There wasn't a word whispered as we drove through the fisherman's village.

Finally reaching a very small cottage at the end of the road, we were in front of the doctor's residence/office that the villagers directed us too. Quickly we got the pilot in there an immediately he was taken back to another room and we were told to wait in the very quaint country like waiting room. It was the first time in years that all of us were able to use a normal bathroom facility and we definitely took advantage of cleaning up and feeling like humans again. The nurse in charge was nice enough to realize we needed some hygiene assistance and she gave us the proper toiletries we needed and told us to feel at home. It was such a quaint little cottage for a doctor's office.

Judy, still upset about the rape nights ago, was the first to use the facilities and she just couldn't scrub hard enough to get the smell of that awful soldier off of her. She literally scubbed herself raw in places. It was such a violent rape as all of us had previously experienced. The only difference was she killed her attacker and got the revenge she needed to go on!

In the meantime, the doctor came out to tell everyone that our pilot was going to recover from his wound and he took the bullet out. However, he would have to remain on IV antibiotics for twenty-four hours before he would let him go. Tina remarked that we really needed to move on quickly but the doctor refused to let her move the pilot. Compromising by saying to her that he understood our situation and he was prepared to help. The cottage, as most village cottages these days, had a secret closet and he took us to it. Opening into a huge one room with cots, blankets, rows of food on the shelves surrounding the room as well as computer and technical equipment. We rejoiced and knew that finally we would fill our bellies with a prepared meal that sat on the table inside this room that the doctor's wife had so graciously cooked for us. We were destined to get a good night's rest but first Tina was interested in getting in touch with her connections to get us out of this country safely. She also would have to get passports and visas which are required to get us through military security checkpoints along the way. Jan, Judy and I were so exhausted we fell asleep, leaving Tina at work and the other standing guard on the room and on our transportation in a shed just barely enough room to keep it securely hidden.

CHAPTER 7

THE NEXT DAY

It seemed like we had just gone to bed when Tina was shaking each of us to wake up. "Hurry" she said. "We must move quietly before we wake the doctor and his wife." The pilot had been on IV antibiotics for 24 hours and was doing much better so the plan was to leave before everyone in the village would be stirring around. As we were moving around in a rush to gather up enough food, supplies and gasoline to last us for a while, the soldiers were getting the pilot situated comfortably in the back of the truck. I felt really bad that we were running out on the only hospitality of real humans with honest intentions but at the same time knew that if we all were going to survive we had to do what was necessary to get us to the nearest airport that would get us out of this country.

According to the map we were about two days from the Donetsk Airport. The very serious downfall to the situation was Tina heard the Ukrainian military were getting ready to seize this airport from the pro-Russian forces. Tina had gathered huge amount of military information and knew we were about to enter an area that would be hard to get through but said she already had contacted her connections. Jan and Judy were very excited to hear there was a plan ready for us to travel to Germany. Once there, we would be home free. I was not as positive as they were because I knew the soldiers would not be allowed to go with us including the pilot and how would Tina cover up that she too was a soldier of the Russian Federation Militia. I kept my intuitions from the girls purposely because I was preparing in my mind how I would get out of this country with my two friends if something happened to Tina. I needed to get my hands on the information that Tina had accumulated from the doctor's residence back in the village. If for no other reason but to read and consume its contents to be ready for anything to happen. We have gotten this far and I am not going to let anything stop us now!

Traveling through the day I kept thinking about my husband and my family. Would they be receptive to me or would Toby be right about my family completely giving up on me? I couldn't believe any of it. All any of us can do is pray to be reunited with our families. I was concerned that all the torturing and drugs they had been through really affected them to the point of losing some memories of their love ones.

We've been on the road now for sixteen hours and we were exhausted so Tina ordered the driver to stop for the night and we would camp out and hide a little closer to the bottom of the mountainside. Judy still does not feel safe around the remaining soldiers so I convinced her to stick by me the rest of the night and not to go off by herself. I really don't think she will have to worry after what she did to the last soldier that raped her!

Tina, Judy, Jan and I stayed in a huddle around a very small fire which was being used to prepare our dinner by one of the soldiers. Jan had checked on the pilot to make sure he was doing okay and gave him his medicines and some warm coffee that was just made on the camp fire along with some soup for him. The pilot was anxious to get up and help the others who would have to stand guard but she talked him into getting another good night's rest and he could see in the morning if he wanted to take on those tasks. She talked softly to him while she changed his bandages, prepared his bed of straw and blankets to keep him warm and protect him from the weather. She went as far as to place a weapon beside him, just in case we were attacked during the night. Jan was skeptical that we would make it to our destination. She expressed concerns to me before she started eating in such a depressed state of mind that I was worried what she might do. Even though she seemed alright taking care of the pilot, I felt I needed to keep watch over her. We all have been through so much since that day ten years ago.

Soon dinner was ready and the hot stew with a chunk of homemade bread from what the doctor's wife had made for us the night before, tasted so good to us! A full moon and a starry sky in the Carpathians Mountains in the winter was the most beautiful winter landscape scene I had ever seen. It was time to wrap up and fall to sleep for another night. This day has been too quiet and who knows what tomorrow will bring.

CHAPTER 8

SECURITY CHECK POINT

Wakening to a very bright sunny day with the weather changing to our advantage, it felt good to get an early start. It was even better to see that the pilot had gotten back on his feet and seemed so grateful to Jan and Judy for helping him get through his healing process. He remarked "Judy did in fact save his life by applying pressure to his wound and Jan just took over like a beautiful Angel from heaven as his nurse." A few more words were exchanged and then Tina announced that we must get moving. We all piled into the back of the truck and began our travels for another day.

We were traveling along when all of a sudden in the distance we could hear gun fire, explosions and see smoke. The driver stopped and said it must be a security check point and they are being attacked. Tina made a mad dash for the artillery as the other soldiers, to include the pilot, took a stand around the vehicle. We were told to stay in the truck and each of us was given a defense weapon to protect ourselves. The driver was sure they hadn't seen us yet so he directed one of the soldiers to move ahead of us to get a closer look at the situation. He was instructed to follow the bottom of the mountainous area and stay out of sight. He must find out if it was the pro-Russian Forces or if it was Toby and his men from the militia.

In the meantime, it was decided by Tina that the driver should go up towards the mountainous areas again and get us off the road. Not only would the truck help to be protection but the huge rocks on the mountainside would be cover for us once again. As we have been fired upon earlier in our travels. It was the roughest ride ever but we were holding on for dear life. Jan began to sob that she knew we wouldn't make it and Judy held her hands and tried to keep her quiet as I prayed for God to find comfort in healing all of us from all the turmoil we have been through and all that we may have to face before we reach the end of our journey.

It seemed like hours before the soldier returned with some very discomforting news. It was Toby and his men who fired upon the security check point and had taken it over. Somehow they had gotten ahead of us around the mountain area on the other side and knew we would have to come through the check point to get through to the airport. I was totally petrified but had to not show it because of Jan's fears. In other words, Toby was one step ahead of me and now it's going to take the action of a full army to take him and his men down. We just did not have enough man or woman power to taken them all down. Tina soon spoke up and said, "This is just what I had expected to happen, so I am prepared for it. You see back at the cottage among all the computer and technical equipment I had access too, I calculated where the first security check point would be and was able to make contact with the remaining forces that are under me to be ready." She continued by saying, "look behind us up further to the mountain top." We did and there before our eyes were soldiers scattered about the mountain top with enough ammunition to even take over the Pro-Russian Forces at the airport. Seems her forces had been following us for some time and she kept it quiet. Tina further remarked, "Toby not only will be captured and the check point taken under siege, but I have made sure he is the first to die by firing squad where we all could watch." Cheering for joy, the three of us were pleased with Tina's actions and cleverness to pull this off.

We were instructed to head for the rocky part of the mountainside to find hiding places and take supplies with us and never come down until she or a member of her forces were to come for us. Tina was taking one soldier and our pilot to travel on foot with her to meet up with her forces and was leaving behind the remaining ones with us. They too would have ammunition from the truck to protect us.

The soldiers that Tina left behind showed no mercy on us. They loaded us up with ammunition and supplies we would need and made sure we knew how to use the weapons. We would have to leave the truck behind because of the steep mountainside. I was beginning to wonder if we would make this hike ourselves with the amount of weight we had to carry. Obviously, there was no time for complaining, we had to do what needed to be done if were going to survive. If, anything ever has been learned so far, it's how to survive!

We made it to the edge of the steep rocky edge and suddenly we were told to lie down in the tall grass and stay very still. What was going on was not for us to be a part of so the two remaining soldiers separated from us and were gone for quite a while. Whey they returned one of the soldiers immediately grabbed Judy and told her put her wrist together as Jan and I watched with a gun pointed at us the other soldier. "What are you doing?" yelled Jan. Quickly she was instructed to shut up! The soldier told Judy to get on her knees and put her hands up on top of the rock. Screaming, she said "No", at which time the soldier tied a band around her mouth and pushed her to the ground. "You bitch, you will pay for killing our friend!" Then telling her that her friend Tina would be in for a big surprise when she reaches the check point. He told us that they were rebel soldiers of the militia and Toby was their leader. He ordered them to kill Jill for what she had done to his soldier and now she would die a slow death. I lunged toward him and the soldier who had us at gun point grabbed me by the hair and said, "I should kill you, but Toby wants you to be brought back to him alive, so now you will be tied up with your friend beside you while you watch the execution of your friend." He immediately gagged the two of us and tied us together so tight there was no way we could move. My heart was in my throat and I could see that Jan was about to pass out. I couldn't see Judy's face but I knew she was petrified. There were so many things going through my head and all I could think of was how much I wished we were back in America safe and this nightmare was just that, a horrible dream! Suddenly the soldier pulled out his machete from his belt and cut of Judy's trigger finger and the one next to it as Jan and I watched in horror. Judy's body quivered and she couldn't make a sound and blood was gushing out like water from a broken water pipe. All I could think of was how she was suffering and the thoughts that must be going through her head. Removing her gag from her mouth, Judy screamed in pain and begged for the soldier to shoot her and get it over with. Again, the soldier laughed and told her that would be too easy of a death for her. What an in humane bastard he was to watch her bleeding, begging and screaming. I prayed for God to put an end to all of this torture and the soldier shot Judy in the head killing her instantly!

When we came too from passing out, Jan and I were untied and in the back of the truck inside of a cage locked up like animals and Jan was crying so deeply she could hardly catch her breath.

What we had just experienced was terrifying and now everything was whirling around in our minds wonderings who would be next. Grieving and holding onto one another, we knew that heading to the security check point would no longer be safe for us as Tina had explained before, she left us behind with these barbaric human beings.

As the truck moved faster and faster, I kept trying to figure how we could get out of this cage but the heavy chains and locks they had around the entire cage were impossible for either one of us to remove. It wasn't long before exhaustion set in and I fell asleep next to Jan who already had cried herself to sleep.

THE BREAK AWAY

A loud noise and sudden stop woke both Jan and I up. We could hear the soldiers talking and seems the noise we heard was from the truck, some kind of mechanical failure. I wanted to laugh because I knew if these two soldiers did not arrive at the security check point when Toby demanded them to be there it would be off with their heads! I refrained from laughing because all I could think about was having lost Judy and wondering what they had done to Tina. My thoughts on making it to the airport were also diminishing as the time was counting down for making the flight that Tina had planned for us to get us out of the Ukraine. Meantime, we heard the truck start up and knew they had fixed whatever was wrong. I was surprised they hadn't checked on us in this awful and very crowded cage. I'm sure their only concern was to get us to Toby fast as they could now.

I knew we needed a distraction to make them stop so I told Jan to start screaming and I would follow as well. Screaming to the top of our lungs for help, again brought the truck to an abrupt stop. The driver orders the other soldier to go back and see what those bitches are screaming about. Naturally when he pulled the canvas back to see what was going on, we told him we had to go to the bathroom and please let us out so we could do that. He hesitated but then started to undo the locks and chains using a key he pulled from his chest pocket. Jan immediately started making gestures with her tongue that made him think he may get somewhere with her if he went with her behind the tall weeds and rocks on the side of the road. He told me to wait and he would be back and he locked me back in. I prayed that Jan would be able to distract enough to get the key from him. After all, what we learned in the underground was these soldiers never lacked for any sex whether they took it or it was freely given to them. Before the soldier left with Jan, he told me to be quiet because the driver was going to take a nap once he knew what was going on.

It seemed like forever before only Jan returned with blood on her hands with the key between her fingers. She had noticed a nice size loose rock when she squatted down to pee and slowly picked it up as she got up and that's when the soldier was caught off guard and she smashed him up side his head knocking him to the ground. Then she stabbed him with his own knife and grabbed the key and his rifle. She had run so fast back to the truck that she was completely out of breath. As she was telling me what had happened, she unlocked the cage and let me out. I took the gun from her and snuck around to the driver's side of the truck and Jan hollered and he jumped out of his seat onto the ground and I shot him.

Now our plans were changing and we had the advantage. With both soldiers dead, we undressed them and put their clothes on so we could not be noticed as women dressed of those from the underground. Jan found a map in the truck that showed and pin pointed where the two soldiers were headed. On the map it showed where the security check point was but it also showed another road to it further to the west of us that would get us there. My theory at this time was Toby, most likely, was getting very anxious about now and his anxiety level was probably going through the roof. I felt he would wait no longer for the soldiers to arrive with us and would take some of his men and set out to find us. If this is true and we took this other route to the west he would not run directly into us and we could have a chance of getting through that check point.

The only thing I could think of was finding Tina alive and with the documents we needed to get us to that plane. I was sure Toby would not do any execution of her without my presence so he could boast to me how I could never get away from him. Jan and I needed to make sure we were not recognizable at all as we approached the check point so Jan found some war paint under the seat of the truck and started to rub her face. She actually did a very good job and with the soldiers helmet you could not tell she was a female. As we continued to travel, Jan applied the war pain on me as if she was a pro at it and we both now looked like the soldiers we left behind. Neither one of us showed any remorse for having killed them. We spent ten years with these bastards and they got what they deserved for torturing and killing Judy.

We followed the road until it ended and we couldn't travel beyond the boulders that were blocking the roadway. I was a little set back thinking it was a trap so we grabbed our weapons and all the ammunition we could carry and headed to the check point about a mile ahead according to the map. Taking this road to the West may have been a mistake due to the dead end but we had to deal with it and move on foot the rest of the way. For the first time in my life I felt I was involved in a war, a war that was determined to destroy life through devastation of trafficking women from all over the world. Jan and I were ready to take on anything we should come in contact with and feeling strong, determined and wanting so much to get to the airport!

ATTACK ON SECURITY CHECK POINT

As we approached the check point ahead, we fell to our knees and crawled behind several rocks to access the situation. Right before our eyes were Tina and the pilot tied to a pole together. The pilot was bleeding from the side of his head and we couldn't tell if he was still alive but Tina was wiggling around like she was trying to get away. There were two guards watching over them and they were sitting down eating some food. If we are going to make a move it would be now. Jan and I looked at each other and both of us knew what we had to do.

Jan made her move first and I followed behind her. Sneaking up to the pole while I kept and eye on the two soldiers, she managed to send a signal to Tina which let her know we were here. I motioned for Jan to put her bayonet on her rifle and head for the two soldiers. She fully understood my gestures and with no hesitation we attacked them and very quickly caught them off guard. The both succumbed to the end of our rifles and we wasted not time in getting to Tina and the pilot. Jan got there first and untied Tina who could hardly talk but let us know what was going on and motioned to us to untie the pilot even though he was out of it. Between the three of us we managed to get away carrying the pilot before the others returned.

The security check point looked like a battle ground but Tina said we don't have time to feel any emotions for the dead civilians we saw laying around. There was a jeep we could use to escape to the airport which was only two more miles ahead. She handed us our passports, security ID's and visa's telling us to not lose them for any reason. They were are lifeline to freedom and we only had one chance to make it to that plane before Toby and his militia showed up. Even though Tina was weak from abuse she took from Toby himself during her capture, she was so full of determination to get us all out of there to include the pilot who was not part of Toby's group. He too would have to escape to freedom but would remain in Germany. Jan again worked on the pilot cleaning his wounds and gave him some water as I drove as fast as I could go while Tina navigated.

I was saying to myself as I saw the airport just ahead, God has answered my prayers. Jan just yelled with excitement and Tina had to settle her down. "We haven't made it through security yet, so be very quiet." With the clothes we have on we were to act like solders delivering two wounded counterparts to Germany for medical assistance. I was to hold on to Tina and Jan was to assist the pilot. One of the security officers quickly approached us as we entered the airport when he saw we needed assistance. He supplied us with two wheel chairs and directed us to our flight gate after he took us through security check himself. It was as if he was part of Tina's plan but how would he know. It didn't matter because now we were ready to board the plane. Tina advised him that we needed to depart immediately and he acknowledged by saying to the pilots" Get this plane in the air" and started to close the walkway up when we heard a commotion way down the airport. "Oh God! It's Toby", I said. About that time the plane was released for takeoff. We hardly got our seatbelts on when we started toward the runway.

RUNWAY TO FREEDOM

J ust as the plane was entering the runway preparing for takeoff at Donetsk Airport, we could see soldiers running towards us shooting at us. Toby was a very desperate man who was not about to give up on capturing me even if it met blowing up the entire plane. Thoughts were going through my mind of him succeeding at getting me off this plane and what he would do to me and the others. It was no secret that by now he would kill everyone in front of me and I would remain alive, living in a hell beyond anybody's imagination.

Everyone was told to drop down in their seats because this plane was going in the air. I could feel the plane moving a little faster and I knew we were going to make it. There was a silence that couldn't be described on the plane and it was then I knew God had answered all our prayers and the plane was in the air.

The attempt to bring us to a stop was unsuccessful and the amazing feeling of heading for freedom just was surreal. The pilot came on and announced the Pro-Russian Forces had just attacked the renegade soldiers from the underground and they all have been killed. We all cheered with joy and now we could breathe with great relief. Jan was crying her heart out as she remembered what had happened to Judy, and Tina assured her that this nightmare was over. Toby Zobar would never be able to sadistically torture, rape or murder another human being again.

We were five hours away from reaching Frankfurt Airport in Frankfurt, Germany and all I could think about was going home and how my family would react to seeing me after all these years. I kept seeing the videos of a woman with my husband that Toby had made me watch and how he seemed so happy with her. Would he even respond to knowing I was alive and coming home? Will my children recognize me? They were only six and four years old when I was kidnapped. My heart is pounding so fast right now and I'm experiencing mix emotions only because of rejection that may happen with my family members.

Tina and the pilot would have to be transported to the hospital in Germany. Jan and I would also have to go through a clear medical check. Tina advised that we would have to go through the American Embassy in Germany to be able to let the families know we were alive and our location. My heart was sinking at the thought of informing Judy's family of her horrible tragedy.

Tina remarked that we were about to face a new world. None of us had knowledge of what was happening in

America today. No matter what we had to face, we could overcome anything after what we had all been through over the past ten years. We definitely had sacrificed and paid the price for our freedom.

Still in the uniforms Jan and I had taken off the two dead soldiers and with war paint on our faces we just couldn't wait for an opportunity to get cleaned up and change in to civilian clothing. We were told by the stewardess on board that someone would be waiting to greet us with the necessary things we would need and when we arrive at hospital with Tina and the pilot, we would be escorted to a non-public area to change. Again, we have Tina to thank for all these arrangements that were being made for us. She certainly has become our hero for someone, who once was on the other side of our underground world terrifying experience.

ARRIVING IN FRANFURT GERMANY

I fell asleep and woke up suddenly when the pilot came over the intercom and advised us to fasten our seat belts. We were about to land and nothing could be more exciting for all of us. Tina already gave each of us our passports and visas so we were ready to depart the plane.

We also would have to get to Consulates Office in Frankfurt as soon as everyone was released from the hospital which hopefully would be the same day.

Looking through the window, I will never forget how beautiful Frankfurt, Germany was from the air. We are about to land at the third largest airport in Europe. Beautiful skyscrapers and the River Main surround the airport. I read in an onboard magazine that Frankfurt is sometimes referred to as Mainhattan, which is spelled differently from our New York Manhattan in the United States. Suddenly reality sets in and tears were beginning to flow.

The anxiety was starting to show on all our faces. We are so close yet so far away from this nightmare being over. As the plane was descending onto the runway there was a quietness about everyone and you could actually hear a pin drop. Not one word was whispered and it was as if we were all in a trance. Our lives would now be so much different than it had been in the past ten years and for us, there would be major life changes, possibly lots of mental therapy to get us through it all.

Departing the plane was a piece of cake and not as hard for us as we all had anticipated. The airport was huge and little overwhelming as we were greeted by emergency personnel to take us all to a huge medical transport. I was so happy that none of us were to be separated, at least for now. The airport was so beautiful and architecturally decorated like we were walking through one of the great Museums that Frankfurt, Germany was known for. Our guardian angel, Judy was watching overt us and guiding us to a safer world.

Within an hour of landing, we were already transported to the hospital and in the process of all of us going through medical attention as planned. Once Jan and I were released we were approached by two uniformed security officers from the hospital and escorted to a private area. It was here that we were given our clothing and accessories to get cleaned up and remove all the war paint from our faces. When I finished, I couldn't believe how great I felt to be able to dress in civilian clothing and to fix my long hair. Using a blow dryer again was like a luxury and using the flat iron they had given to me was a real challenge as this was as strange piece of equipment to me. There were two ladies in our dressing area who were helping us. One of them showed me how to use it and ended up actually doing it for me. It was an amazing transformation for my very difficult styling hair in the past. The other lady was helping Jan adjust to hair styling as well. It was like we were about to make a debut into an audience of some kind. We both felt like knew human beings and excited to be safe again.

We asked to see Tina and the pilot so we could check on their conditions. Tina was about to be released herself and couldn't wait to get transformed like us. The bad news was the pilot would remain in the hospital because his wounds needed more medical attention than we thought. He needed to have more IV antibiotics for several days to clear infections before they would release him and his family had been notified already.

Once we got Tina taken care of, we were all ready to conquer our new beginnings and we said our goodbyes to the pilot. We would cherish the moments we spent with this man and how he placed his own life in danger to save ours. A memory we would never forget. It was time now for us to go on to the next phase of our process to get back to America. The hospital security guards were ready to take us to be transported to a hotel where we would spend time before we met the Consulate.

CHAPTER 13

AN UNEXPECTED SURPISE

Time just seemed to be going in slow motion but there were so many steps to go through as we were given instructions on what would happen next. Tina seemed nervous at the hotel and made sure we all stayed together as we were escorted to the most beautiful dining area I had ever seen before in my life. The restaurant's architectural design was dramatically modern, the dining room was inside a glass box overlooking the Rhine River. The view just took our breaths away as we were seated at a huge table surrounded by contemporary columns. The strange part about all of this was the entire room was completely empty of people accept us. I noticed a small podium with a microphone setting on a ceramic tile platform and there was soft music flowing through speakers surrounding the entire room.

We were prepared for a meal fit for a Queen and that's exactly how we were treated. Our servers were kind and generous to us as they made their way through the entire dinner. I was starting to feel a sense of something amazing about to happen when I looked up and saw a stocky gentleman with distinctive white hair standing at the podium about to speak. He introduced himself as the Consulate and welcomed us to the most beautiful city in Germany and gave us a little history lesson at the same time. The atmosphere was like a special awards ceremony in the making. Suddenly the lights from the chandeliers above us dimmed and all we could see were shadows in the background. Jan and I were in a state of shock from all of this and were about to get the surprise of our lives.

Tina had such great connections from her years of experience in the field of communications but we never dreamed she could arrange what was about to take place right before our eyes. I noticed silhouettes of people in the background behind the podium but I couldn't make out who they were and why they were there. The Consulate himself choked up a little as he welcomed again another group to the occasion, a group of people who had been flown to Frankfurt by support of the American Embassy of Germany to be reunited with their loved ones after ten years of never having given up hope that someday this would become reality.

Jan, Tina and I all three, at the same time shouted " Oh My God, it's our families" and with that one by one we were greeted by each of them. I couldn't believe how my children had grown as I caressed them in my arms and we were all crying. They had grown up so much and oh how I longed for this day. Then my husband Jim, who looked almost the same as the day I last saw him, put his arms around me and squeezed me so tight I thought I was going to lose my breath. "Annette, he said, "I have waited so long to hold you in my arms and never gave up on searching for you." Then it hit me, where was his girlfriend that Toby had showed me videos of and so convinced me that Jim had completely given up on ever seeing me again? Then in a split second I let it go as I just engulfed myself in hugging and kissing my family and being reunited with them.

I could hear Jan and Tina's excitement as they too were being greeted with their loved ones. It was such a treasured moment for all of us and our families. Our concentration was then interrupted again in a very soft voice by the Consulate for all of us to please take seats. In his ending speech for the evening he assured us that all of us would have accommodations free of charge for our families for the next few days here in Frankfurt to further become acquainted with our families. Then he said we would all able to fly back to the United States together and to our homes where he hoped we would be able to adjust and overcome the tragic events of the past ten years of all our lives. His last words were for our dear friend Judy who had suffered a tortuous death at the hands of such evil and cowardly soldiers who in turn got what they deserved from the revenge upon them by her three dearest friends Jan, Tina and Annette (who was known as ANNA BELLA to them at the time). As he directed us in a moment of prayer, the room became silent and for the first time I felt Judy's presence once again whispering to me that we all would meet again someday but for now peace in our hearts and keep our loved ones close and never let them go.

www.ingramcontent.com/pod-product-compliance
Lightning Source LLC
Chambersburg PA
CBHW050428110726
47899CB00008B/2896